Back to School, Mallory

For Ellen Stein, editor extraordinaire...
and a fabulous friend
—L.F.

For Addison
—T.S.

Back to School, Mallory

by Laurie Friedman

illustrations by Tamara Schmitz

Carolrhoda Books, Inc. / Minneapolis

CONTENTS

A WORD FROM MALLORY

My name is Mallory McDonald (like the restaurant, but no relation), age eight and almost 3/4. Until two months ago, my life was perfect. Nothing awful had ever happened to me.

Until my parents made me move to a new town. I had to get used to a new house, a new room and, worst of all, a new best friend. It was really, really, really hard.

Now my parents want me to start third grade at a new school. And guess what they want me to bring with me ... MY MOM!

When I found out she was hired to be the new music teacher at Fern Falls Elementary, I had what Dad calls a Mallory Meltdown (it sounds like an ice cream sundae, but trust me ... it's not!).

6

"Mom can't go to school with me!" I screamed. "Kids take notebooks and pencils and rulers and erasers to school, but they don't take their moms!"

Mom looked at me calmly. "Some kids do."

"But I don't want to be one of them!" I stamped my feet and shook my head. "It's hard enough being the new kid. I don't want to be the new kid who brings her mom with her!"

Mom just looked at me and shook her head.

"Please!" I begged. "Can't we at least talk about it?"

"Mallory," Mom said. "There's nothing to talk about. Come Monday morning, you and I are going to Fern Falls Elementary— TOGETHER!"

And that's when I got a feeling . . . a taking-my-mom-to-school-with-me-doesn't-seem-like-a-good-way-to-start-third-grade feeling.

I'm sunk. I'm doomed. I'm dead meat. And I haven't even started school yet.

A BAD START

Someone sits down on my bed and rubs my back. "Guess who?" says a voice.

Even though I'm covered with covers, I don't have to guess. I know it's Mom.

She tickles my back. "Rise and shine, Sleepyhead. Summer vacation is officially over." Then she whispers in my ear. "I have a back-to-school surprise for you. I'm making chocolate chip pancakes— your favorite!"

Mom always has a surprise for me on

the first day of school. I think she thinks that's what it takes to get me excited about going back to school. I usually am excited, but today is different.

"I have a surprise for you too," I tell Mom. I stick my hand out of the covers and hand her a sheet of paper. "Read!" I say.

Mom is quiet for a minute, and then she clears her throat and starts reading.

10 Reasons Why I, Mallory McDonald, Can NOT Go to School Today.

REASON #1: There are lots of germs at school. I could get sick.

REASON #2: The water fountain might explode, and I could get wet.

REASON #3: A big, fat, mean, ugly fifth grader might step on my toe and crush it.

REASON #4: I could get food poisoning if I eat lunch in the cafeteria.

REASON #5: It might snow, and school would be canceled anyway.

REASON #6: Max would like it better if I stayed home and so would Cheeseburger who will be one very, very, very lonely cat without me.

REASON #7: Someone should be home in case we get a delivery.

REASON #8: If I stay home, I will rake the front yard. (I Promise!)

REASON #9: I'm pretty smart and probably don't need to go to Third Grade.

REASON #10: Even if I do, I want to be homeschooled.

Mom sighs. "Mallory, going to a new school is scary. And I know you're not happy I'm going with you, but if you'll give it a chance, I'm sure everything will work out fine."

She rubs my back through the covers. "You'll get used to the new school, and before you know it, you'll forget all about your old school."

"BRRNNNK!" I make a sound like a buzzer going off in a game show when the person on stage gets the answer wrong. "I'll never forget about my old school!"

Or my old best friend, Mary Ann. She has Mrs. Thompson this year.

Mrs. Thompson is the nicest third-grade teacher on the planet. She keeps a candy jar on her desk with a note taped to it: *"Take one if you're having a bad day."*

Mary Ann and I have been waiting since

kindergarten to have her, and now Mary Ann has her . . . without me. It's not fair! I pull my blanket in around me.

Mom tries to pull the covers off of me. "C'mon, Mallory, we both have to go to school. What do you say we start the year off right by being on time the first day?"

But there's only one thing I have to say: "I'M NOT GOING TO SCHOOL TODAY!"

Mom stops pulling. "Sweet Potato, I'm sure with Mrs. Daily as your teacher, today will be a good day." Mom chuckles. "In fact, I think with Mrs. Daily, good things will happen on a daily basis. Get the joke? Mrs. Daily. Daily basis."

I get it. And I love jokes, but lately, I haven't been in the mood. I don't move.

"C'mon," says Mom. "Joey's in your class. There's another good thing."

I'm happy Joey's in my class. We've had a lot of fun since I moved in next door to him. But I wish he could be in my class in my old school . . . not in a new school.

Mom pats my covered-up head. "Five minutes," she says in her *I-mean-business* voice. "I don't want your back-to-school surprise to get cold."

"OK, OK," I mumble. When Mom leaves, I tumble out of bed and head for my bathroom. But when I look in the mirror, I get another surprise.

This surprise is purple and glittery and it's all over my face!

I rub the sleepies out of my eyes and put my face up to the mirror for a closer look. Do I have chicken pox? No . . . I HAVE PURPLE GLITTER POX! I feel my head to see if I have a fever. And that's when I see the problem—my fingernails!

I polished them last night with the purple glitter polish Mary Ann gave me. Purple glitter polish is everywhere . . . except on my nails. I must have fallen asleep on my hands before my nails were dry. I can't go to school like this!

I race up the stairs to Mom's bathroom to get the polish remover. I pull bottles and jars out of her cabinet. I find the bottle I'm looking for—but it's empty!

What am I going to do?

I try rubbing my purple glitter pox off. I try scrubbing my purple glitter pox off. I even put my face in the bathroom sink and try soaking my purple glitter pox off.

Now my face is red and blotchy *and* purple and glittery.

I can just see my third-grade scrapbook. The first picture in it won't be pretty.

"Mallory, hurry up!" Mom calls from the kitchen. "You don't want to be late for your first day of school."

Actually, I do. I would love to be late. A whole year late.

I pull on capris and my best purple T-shirt. *What am I going to do?*

Then, I know. I know *exactly* what I'm going to do. I search through my closet until I find my ski mask. I pull it on and look in the mirror. Not bad. All you can see are my eyes, nose, and mouth. I will be the mystery girl of third grade.

"MALLORY!"

I pull my ski mask down a little further and head to the kitchen.

I sit down at the table and take a bite of pancakes. "Mmmm."

My brother Max looks at me like someone told a joke and he's the only one who didn't get it. "Why are you wearing a ski mask?"

"It's a new style." I take another bite. "A lot of third graders are doing it."

Max grabs my mask. "None that I know."

I try to keep my mask on, but Max is too fast. He stares at my face like he's just seen a two-headed zebra. "Mom! Dad! Look at Mallory!"

Mom drops her fork. Dad puts his newspaper down.

Now I know how the monkeys at the zoo must feel. Everyone is staring . . . AT ME! "We have to go to the drugstore before

school starts and buy some polish remover."

Mom shakes her head. "We don't have time to go to the store before school."

I pull my ski mask back on. "I can't go to school with purple dots on my face!"

Max yanks it off. "She can't go to school with a ski mask on either."

Mom inspects my face. "It's not that bad. You're going to school and the ski mask is staying home. That's final." She picks up her notebook. "School is waiting."

"Not so fast," says Dad. He pulls a camera out of a drawer. "Time for the McDonald family back-to-school picture."

Max groans. "Dad, not this year."

For once, I agree with Max.

Dad shakes his head, "It's tradition. Max, Mallory, over by the piano. Sherry, you too. After all, you're going back to school too."

Mom puts her arms around Max and me. "Smile," says Dad. He snaps our picture.

But as I follow Mom out the door, all I can think is that I don't have much to smile about. This day will go down as one of the worst ever. There will even be pictures to remind me of my horrible start to third grade.

Next door Joey and his dog, Murphy, are waiting for us in his front yard. Joey's sister, Winnie, and his dad, Mr. Winston, and his grandpa are there too.

"What happened to you?" Winnie looks at me like I'm contagious.

"You don't want to know," I mumble.

Joey studies my face like he's trying to figure out a tricky problem in math. "I have a ski mask if you want to borrow it."

Max laughs and tells Joey I don't need a ski mask.

Joey shrugs. "At least your face matches your shirt and your backpack. Everyone will know what your favorite color is as soon as they meet you."

Joey's dad smiles. "An excellent way of looking at things."

Mom starts down the sidewalk. "We're off to school!" she says. Winnie and Max follow Mom. Joey pats Murphy's head and falls in line. "We're off to school!"

I follow Joey. "We're off," I mumble.

But there's only one thing I'm off to . . . A BAD START!

HIDE-N-PEEK

There are lots of things I can't do with my head inside my backpack. Like find the way to my classroom. Even though Joey is guiding me through the maze of feet and stray notebooks, I have to work hard not to trip.

Joey stops. "There's a sign on the door." He reads out loud. "Mrs. Daily, Room 310. Welcome to Third Grade."

I can't believe I'm starting third grade in hiding. But I can just imagine what kids would say if they could see my face.

"Check out the new kid."

"What's with the purple dots?"

"Where's she from? Jupiter?"

I don't want anybody to think I'm from another planet! My head's inside my backpack, and that's where it's staying.

"Good morning, class," says Mrs. Daily. "Please find the desk with your name tag on it and take a seat."

I move my backpack, just a little, so I can find the desk with the *Mallory McDonald* sticker. When I stick my name tag on my T-shirt, it goes on lopsided.

I sit down and peek at the girl in the chair next to me. She has on a rainbow T-shirt, matching glasses, and a perfectly straight name tag.

I wish Joey was in the chair next to me. But his desk is across the room next to another boy. I try to get his attention, but he doesn't see me. He's busy talking to the boy in the desk next to him.

Mrs. Daily taps a little green plastic frog on her desk. It croaks, and everyone stops talking. Mrs. Daily smiles and picks up the frog. "Class, this is Chester. When he opens his mouth, you will know it is time to close yours."

Great. Mary Ann's teacher keeps candy on her desk. Mine has a croaking frog.

Mrs. Daily keeps smiling. "The seat you are sitting in will be yours for the year. Let's all take a minute and introduce ourselves to our desk mates."

The girl in the rainbow T-shirt knocks on my backpack. "Anybody home?"

"Mallory McDonald. Like the restaurant, but no relation."

My desk mate leans over and peeks

inside my backpack. "Pamela Brooks. Why are you wearing a backpack on your head on the first day of school?"

I pull my head out of my backpack so Pamela can see my purple glitter pox.

She studies my face like she's a doctor and I'm getting a checkup. "You look better without the backpack."

I hope Pamela is right. I slide my backpack under my desk.

"OK, class," says Mrs. Daily. "Now that we know our desk mates, let's get to know each other. When it's your turn, please say your name and share something about yourself with the class. Who would like to start?"

Pamela raises her hand.

Mrs. Daily checks her seating chart. "Thank you for volunteering, Pamela."

Pamela stands up. "Hi everybody, my name is Pamela Brooks. I want to be a famous journalist when I grow up."

"You're in the right classroom." Mrs. Daily smiles. "We'll be doing a lot of writing this year. Our class is in charge of the school newspaper."

Mrs. Daily checks her seating chart. "Mallory, you're next."

I stand up. "My name is Mallory McDonald."

"She likes purple," says a voice.

There's giggling all around me.

I feel like I need to say why my face is purple. The problem is I don't want to say why it's *really* purple. Mary Ann would say this calls for some creative sharing.

I clear my throat. "This morning, I was polishing my cat's toenails when she started jumping all over the place."

I move my arms around to show what a wild, jumping cat looks like. "When I tried to calm her down, I got polish all over my face."

I turn around in a circle so everyone can see my purple dots. "I didn't want to be late on the first day of school, so I had to leave it on."

There's more giggling.

Mrs. Daily taps Chester's head. "Class, that's enough. Mallory moved here this summer and brought someone special to school with her. Mallory, why don't you tell the class who in your family is part of Fern Falls Elementary now."

"My mother is the new music teacher," I mumble.

"Mrs. McDonald has some wonderful plans for music this year," says Mrs. Daily. "You'll hear more when you meet Mrs. McDonald later this week."

Everybody stares at me. I wonder if this is how it's going to be all year . . . *Mallory McDonald, daughter of the music teacher.*

I try to pay attention while Mrs. Daily continues with the introductions.

Zack likes tomato sandwiches. Adam went to school in South Africa for a year. Sammy hates being the oldest because he gets blamed for everything. Emma collects rubber bands, glow rocks, and used paper. Grace collects shoes.

I try to remember who likes tomato sandwiches and who collects used paper, but my mind keeps thinking about my face and my mom.

Mrs. Daily calls on two girls who are desk mates.

Danielle and Arielle are Virgos and best friends.

They're lucky. They're best friends, *and* they're desk mates. I wonder who Mary Ann's desk mate is this year. I wonder if they'll become best friends.

Mrs. Daily calls on Joey. "I like skateboarding and soccer," says Joey.

His desk mate is Pete. "I like skateboarding and soccer too," says Pete. When Pete sits down, he and Joey high-five each other.

It looks like Joey likes his desk mate.

Nicholas, Brittany, Evan, April, Dawn, and Jackson introduce themselves. There are lots of names to remember.

Mrs. Daily spends the rest of the morning telling us about some of the units we'll be studying this year. Bears. Pilgrims. The United States of America.

When the lunch bell rings, we line up and follow Mrs. Daily to the cafeteria.

Someone behind me groans. I think it's a *we're-too-old-to-have-to-line-up-behind-the-teacher-and-walk-to the-cafeteria* groan. But I'm glad we do. I have no idea where the cafeteria is at this school. In my old school, I knew where everything was. I knew what to do. I even knew who to sit with at lunch. At this school, I have no idea.

When I get inside the cafeteria, I sit down next to Joey.

"Boys' table." He shrugs his shoulders. "Sorry."

I can't believe Joey doesn't want to eat lunch with me. Friends are supposed to eat lunch with friends. I always ate lunch with Mary Ann.

I pick up my lunch bag and go sit at the table with the girls from my class. But I feel like I should call it the *I-don't-have-anybody-to-talk-to-because-everybody-is-already-talking-to-somebody-else* table.

I unwrap my sandwich and take a bite. But when I do, I taste something awful . . . tuna fish! Max always gets tuna fish, and I always get peanut butter and marshmallow. Mom gave me the wrong sandwich on the first day of school!

I take another bite of tuna fish and gag.

I'm not sure if it's the tuna fish or every single thing about this day, but I'm starting to feel sick.

After lunch, Mrs. Daily gives us our first spelling list: *elbow, groans, shadows, bulldozer, coast, loan, cobra, over.*

I wish a bulldozer would run over me.

Two hours and forty-nine minutes until I'll be through with this day.

"Class," Mrs. Daily says. "We have a lot to look forward to this week. Tuesdays will be art days. So tomorrow, you'll have your first art class. On Wednesdays, you'll have P.E. And on Thursdays, music. This Thursday, you'll meet Mrs. McDonald."

When Mrs. Daily says "This Thursday, you'll meet Mrs. McDonald," everyone turns around and looks at me.

I groan. I wish I could run. I wish I could hide. I wish I could be anywhere but here right now . . . even Jupiter.

SINGING THE
BLUES

I'm on a mission . . . a *Thursday-morning-make-a-wish-before-school* mission.

I live on a street called Wish Pond Road. There's a real wish pond on my street. I can throw stones into it and make all the wishes I want.

When I moved to Wish Pond Road, Joey told me that the shiny black stones are wish pebbles. He said if you find one, your wish will come true.

The only problem is that wish pebbles are hard to find.

I pick up a plain, white rock and throw it into the water. *I wish everybody will like my mom when they meet her today.*

I watch the pond water ripple where I threw in the stone.

I think back to Tuesday when we had art with Mrs. Pearl.

"We're going to have so much fun in art this year," she said. She told us that as third graders, we'd be studying lots of different kinds of art. Then she wrote the word *expressionism* on the board and explained what it meant.

"Expressionism is a type of art where the artist paints what he's feeling inside, not necessarily what things really look like in the outside world."

Mrs. Pearl held up a picture of some flowers. "This is a painting called 'Sunflowers' by a famous expressionist artist named Vincent Van Gogh."

Mrs. Pearl passed out paper and showed us how to sketch flowers. She said we'd be talking a lot about expressing ourselves through our artwork.

"Isn't Mrs. Pearl nice?" Pamela said as we walked back to Room 310.

I throw another rock into the water. Pamela was right. Mrs. Pearl is nice.

On Wednesday, we had P.E. with Coach Kelly.

When we got to the field, Coach Kelly blew his whistle. "No time like the present to get in shape." We lined up and did stretches and jumping jacks.

"You look like a bunch of professional athletes," said Coach Kelly.

Then he told us we were in training to run the mile. We ran laps around the track. He high-fived everybody as we passed him.

"Isn't Coach Kelly cool?" Joey whispered to me.

I throw another rock in the wish pond. *Everybody* likes Mrs. Pearl and Coach Kelly. I hope when everybody meets my mom today, they feel the same way about her.

"MALLORY!" Mom calls my name from down the street.

As I walk home, I think about what Mom said last night. She promised me she would do her best to be my mom at home and my music teacher at school. But Max told me I shouldn't count on that promise.

"Mallory, Mom is the music teacher. You're going to have to face the music." He laughed like crazy. "Get the joke?"

I got it. Even though Max said he

doesn't see what the big deal is about Mom teaching at our school, to me IT IS A VERY BIG DEAL!

So today I'm doing everything I can to make sure there's nothing to laugh about when the Fern Falls Elementary third graders meet my mom.

I made wishes at the wish pond. I'm wearing my four-leaf clover charm bracelet. I have on my lucky leopard socks, even though they're making the walk to school a hot and itchy one.

"Earth to Mallory," says Joey as we follow my mom to school.

"Huh?" I bend down to scratch my ankle.

"We're halfway to school," says Joey. "And you haven't said a word."

I slow down so Mom can't hear what I'm about to say. "I'm a little worried about everyone meeting my mom."

"How bad can it be?" asks Joey.

But that's just it. I don't know how bad it can be. I tried to talk to Mom last night about being nice like Mrs. Pearl or cool like Coach Kelly, but I don't think she was listening.

I think about Van Gogh. I wonder if he ever tried to express himself and nobody listened. I wonder if his mother was a teacher at his school.

As we walk into our classroom, Mrs. Daily tells everyone to take a seat. "We have a busy day," she says.

First, we say the Pledge of Allegiance. Then Mrs. Daily passes out our vocabulary worksheets. "If you don't know what any of the words mean, you can look them up in the dictionary in the back of the room."

One of our words is *nervous.*

I don't need a dictionary to know what *nervous* means.

"Class," says Mrs. Daily, when we're done with our worksheets. "I'm going to walk you down to the music room now. You're going to meet Mrs. McDonald. Please show her how well behaved Fern Falls Elementary

third graders are. Does anybody have any
questions before we go?"

I do. Can we learn long division instead?

"I can't wait to meet your mom," Pamela
whispers in my ear.

When we walk into the music room,
Mom tells everyone to take a seat. "Good
morning, class." Mom smiles. "Welcome to
music. I'm Mrs. McDonald."

But when Mom says *Mrs. McDonald,*
everyone turns around and looks at me.
I wish I could hide my head inside a
songbook.

"We're going to have a lot of fun in
music this year," Mom says. "We'll be
putting on a special show at the end of
October called Fall Festival."

Mom pauses. I think she's waiting for
everyone to clap or cheer.

They might have clapped if she'd said:

We're going to have a lot of fun in music this year. We'll be going to a special concert for kids. It will be an all-day field trip with pizza and ice cream. But that's not what she said.

I think about how things used to be before we moved to Fern Falls. Mom gave piano lessons at home. Even though I had to walk around with cotton balls in my ears, I wish things were like they used to be.

"We're going to start the year off singing 'America,'" says Mom. "I want you to really think about what you're singing." Then she says the words really slowly like she's talking to a room full of two-year-olds.

My coun-try 'tis of thee,
Sweet land of li-ber-ty;
Of thee I sing.

Land where my fa-thers died
Land of the pil-grims' pride
From e-ver-y moun-tain side
Let free-dom ring.

She asks everybody to focus on the song
and repeat the words with her.
I try to focus on *My Country 'Tis of Thee.*
But the words *My Mom Embarrasses Me* just
keep popping into my head.

STREET FRIENDS

"Pass the Fruity Pops," says Mom.

Max and I look at each other. Mom never eats Fruity Pops.

Dad slides the box across the breakfast table. "You've only been at school for a week, and you're already eating like a kid," he says.

Mom laughs.

But I don't. Mom might be eating like a kid, but she's definitely not acting like one. This week at school, she did lots of things kids would NEVER do.

In the girls' bathroom, she reminded everybody to wash their hands. And in the cafeteria, she told the girls to be sure and eat their *healthies* first.

Kids NEVER do either of those things! It's no fun to be the kid whose mother reminds other kids to do that kind of stuff.

"I have good news," says Mom. "We're having dinner at the Winston's tonight."

That is good news, and I know someone else who will think so too. "Lucky Max." I make a kissy face. "He gets to see Winnie."

Max tries to hit me on the head with a cereal box, but the phone rings, and I grab it before Max can get to me.

"Hey! Hey! Hey!" says a voice on the other end.

It's Mary Ann!

"Hey! Hey! Hey!" I sit on top of the desk

and cross my legs. This is a great way to start my Saturday.

"How's school?" I ask Mary Ann.

Mary Ann tells me about Mrs. Thompson and her candy jar. She says third grade is awesome. She says school is the same as last year, only better.

"How's school for you?" Mary Ann asks.

Nothing is the same for me. Different school. Different friends. Different teachers, and Mom is one of them.

I tell Mary Ann about Fern Falls Elementary and Pamela and Mrs. Daily. Then I cover the phone with my hand. "Guess what? Mom is the music teacher at my school," I say in a soft voice.

Mary Ann giggles into the phone. "What's it like having your mom as a teacher?"

"I can't really talk now," I whisper into the phone. "But so far, not so good."

"Gotcha," says Mary Ann. "I can't really talk now either. Emily, Ellen, and Becca are coming over. We have to make a reptile collage for school."

I feel like my Fruity Pops are doing forward rolls in my stomach. If I still lived there, I'd be making a reptile collage at Mary Ann's house too. But the only kind of collage I can make is a "No Friends" collage.

"Have fun." I try to sound cheery as I tell Mary Ann good-bye. But when I hang up the phone, I make an *I-don't-feel-cheery* face.

Dad walks over to the desk. "Mallory, What's the matter? It's a beautiful Saturday morning, and you don't seem your usual sunny self."

"I'm not my usual self," I say. "My usual self would be at Mary Ann's house working on a project with all my friends. But I'm stuck here with no friends."

"Why don't you call Joey?" says Dad. "He's your friend."

"Joey has soccer practice."

"How about one of the other kids in your class," Mom says. "What about your desk mate, Pamela? Why don't you call her and see if she wants to come over."

I shake my head. "I hardly know Pamela."

Mom sits down in front of me. "If you

call her, you'll get to know her."

I groan. Mom can be so predictable. I should have known she'd say something like that.

"Why don't we spend the day together?" I say to Mom. "We can do mother-daughter things, like paint our nails and go out for lunch."

Mom smiles. "I would love to, but I have lesson plans to do and I have to work on Fall Festival. It's right around the corner."

Mom pats my head. "You understand, don't you?"

I understand. I understand that now that Mom has two hundred students, she doesn't have time for her own two kids.

I go into my room and close the door. "Cheeseburger, it's just you and me today." I rub the fur behind her ears.

I think about what Dad said, about not

being my sunny self. I pick up Cheeseburger and stand in front of the mirror in my bathroom. "Cheeseburger," I say out loud. "I proclaim today 'Let's Try Our Hardest to be Sunny' day."

We sit on the bed, and I paint my toenails. Then I get out the scrapbooks Mary Ann and I made. We always worked on our scrapbooks on the weekends.

I think about Joey.

I can't see him doing scrapbooks. He's too busy playing soccer and skateboarding. Even though we like to do some things together, we don't like doing *everything* together, the way Mary Ann and I did.

I flip through the pages of the second-grade scrapbook Mary Ann and I made. "A lot has changed since last year, hasn't it?" I say to Cheeseburger. But when I look

at her, her eyes are closed. I think trying to
be sunny made her sleepy.

After lunch, I read and watch TV until
Mom says it's time to get ready to go over
to the Winston's house.

When we get to their house, Joey opens
the door before we even ring the doorbell.

"What took you so long?" he asks. "I've
got something to show you." Max and I

28 Apr 05

follow Joey into the kitchen. Winnie is at the kitchen table surrounded by piles of playing cards. She's feeding them into a little machine.

"What's that?" I ask.

Winnie rolls her eyes like she's not surprised that I don't know what it is.

"It's an automatic card shuffler," says Joey. "You put the cards in, and the machine does all the shuffling. Dad ordered it for us off the Internet."

"Cool," says Max.

"Very cool," says Joey. "Do you guys want to play Crazy Eights?"

"I don't know how," I tell him. "But I can play Go Fish. Can we play that instead?"

Joey nods. "It's not my favorite, but we can play it if you want."

Winnie rolls her eyes again, but she and Joey and Max and I play Go Fish until Mr. Winston says it's time for dinner.

We eat pizza and make our own sundaes.

During dessert, Joey's grandpa asks about school. "So is the school year off to a good start for you youngsters?" he asks.

"It's OK." Joey shrugs his shoulders. "I like summer better."

"It's great!" Winnie smiles at her grandfather. "Now that we're in fifth grade, Max and I get our own lockers and we get to change classes. Max is in my math class. Don't you think Mrs. Mansberg is the world's *best* math teacher?" Winnie asks Max.

Max swallows a spoonful of strawberry

ice cream and nods his head. "The best,"
he says.

Someone must have squirted whipped
cream in my ears. I'm definitely hearing
things. All Max ever says is that Mrs.
Mansberg is the *worst* teacher in the school.
I think Winnie could say fried eggs taste
good on ice cream and Max would agree
with her.

After dessert, we say good night and go
home. Mom tells Max and me to brush our
teeth and get ready for bed.

I put on my panda bear pajamas and go
into the bathroom to brush my teeth. Max
is already at the sink.

I squeeze some toothpaste onto my
toothbrush. "World's *best* night, huh?"

Max spits. "I guess so."

I guess so. "I can't believe you didn't
think it was super. Winnie was sooooo

friendly." I bat my eyes. "Maybe she likes you as much as you like Mrs. Mansberg."

Max wipes his mouth with a towel. "For your information, she does like me . . . on the street and when no one else is around. At school, she acts like she doesn't even know I'm in her math class."

He tosses the towel in the hamper. "That's what you call a *street friend.*"

I turn off the tap. "I've never heard of a street friend."

"Learn something new every day."

I think about Joey.

He sits at the boys' table in the cafeteria. He goes to soccer practice on the weekends. On Thursday, when Mrs. Daily had us pick partners for a science project, Joey picked Pete.

The only time he really plays with me is when we're together on our street. And when we're on our street, he's really nice. Like tonight, he even played the card game I wanted to play.

"You don't think Joey is my street friend, do you?"

Max shrugs. "Like sister, like brother, if you ask me."

If you ask me, making new friends isn't easy. I hope Max is wrong about Joey. I go into my room and get into bed. I can't sleep, so I try counting sheep. But I end up counting friends instead.

And the trouble is . . . I don't get very far.

STARS EVERYWHERE

"Class, take your seats please," says Mom. "I have some exciting news."

I groan. One of the cool parts about having your mom as a teacher is you know what she's going to say before everybody else does. One of the not-so-cool parts is that you know when she's going to say something that nobody will think is cool.

Today is one of those days.

"As many of you know," Mom says. "The third grade at Fern Falls Elementary always puts on Fall Festival. This year's show is *Down on the Farm*."

I hear giggles from the back of the classroom. Someone whispers, "Mrs. McDonald had a farm."

I knew it! This show is *way* too babyish. At dinner last night, I tried to tell Mom that *Down on the Farm* is too babyish for third graders. Max laughed and said third graders *are* babyish.

Mom said it would be a great show.

She waits for the giggling to stop before she continues. "Fall Festival will be bigger and better than ever. We're going to put together committees to work on costumes, sets, lighting, and makeup."

Pete raises his hand. "When is the show?"

"At the end of October," says Mom. "So we have a lot to do to get ready."

Danielle and Arielle raise their hands. "Can we be in charge of makeup?"

"I'll keep you two in mind," Mom says.

Pamela raises her hand. "I think Fall Festival will be a lot of fun. I can't wait to work on sets and costumes."

Mom smiles at Pamela. "I'm glad you're excited."

All teachers, including my own mother, spend a lot of time smiling at Pamela.

Mom takes a cowboy hat out of the closet and says, "*Down on the Farm* is the story of Farmer Brown and his wife. They grow fruits and vegetables on their farm. Farmer Brown tries selling his fruits and vegetables to the townspeople, but no one wants to buy them. They would rather eat pizza and hamburgers."

Mom continues. "Farmer Brown is upset. He doesn't know what to do. Mrs. Brown comes up with a plan.

"She invites everyone in the town to a giant feast made from the fruits and vegetables they grow on the farm. The food tastes so delicious, the townspeople start buying everything, and Farmer Brown is happy."

Mom holds the cowboy hat in the air.

"Now, we're going to draw to see who will have which roles. Line up," Mom says. "And remember, this is about working together to make a great show. All of the roles are important."

Even though I think this show is kind of stupid, I hope I get a good role.

Joey picks first. He waves a little piece of paper in the air. "I'm Farmer Brown!"

I never thought of Joey as an actor, but he looks happy about his role.

Arielle and Danielle pick next. They both get to be rain fairies. I don't know how they always get to do everything together.

Everyone draws slips of paper out of the hat. There are lots of good parts: farmhands and townspeople. There are lots of not-so-good parts too: fruits and vegetables.

When it's my turn to pick, I cross my toes and make a wish. *Please let me be Mrs. Brown.* I stick my hand in the hat and pull out a piece of crumpled-up paper. I uncrumple it. I'm not Mrs. Brown. I'm an . . . *eggplant.*

I don't want to be an eggplant! I would rather be an apple or a potato. An eggplant has to be the worst role in the show.

Pamela picks next. "Mrs. Brown," she yells. "I get to be Farmer Brown's wife!"

It's not fair! Pamela is Mrs. Brown and I'm an eggplant! I sit down, unroll the sliver of paper in my hand, and read it again.

Brittany looks over my shoulder. "You're an eggplant. I'm a bowl of cherries."

"It's the pits, isn't it?"

Brittany doesn't laugh. "It's going to be

really fun. Making our costumes and all
that other stuff your mom said. Who cares
what role you have?"

I do. I take my paper over to Mom and
tap her on the shoulder. "Uh, Mom, I
mean, Mrs. McDonald." I'm not even sure
what to call my own mom. "I need to

redraw," I whisper in her ear. "I don't want to be an eggplant."

"You'll make a fine eggplant," Mom whispers in my ear. She tells me to sit down. Then she asks everyone to take their seats.

I can't believe it. My own mom won't let

me redraw. I'm her daughter, and she's treating me like I'm just another kid. This is so unfair!

Pamela passes a note folded into a neat square to me. I open it up.

Mallory, I'm so excited!!! I can't believe I get to be the farmer's wife.

Are you:

A. So excited about your part?

B. Going to work on the costume committee?

C. Feeling like this is going to be the best Fall Festival ever?

I'm all three!!! Pamela

I consider Pamela's note for about two seconds. I know Pamela is A, B, and C. But

I'm D . . . none of the above. I DON'T WANT ANY PART OF THIS SHOW.

I shove Pamela's note in my pocket. I think about what Mom said, about giving Pamela a chance. I'm trying, but that's hard to do when she does things that annoy me, like writing this silly note.

Mary Ann and I used to pass notes, but that was different because she used to pass notes I liked reading.

When the bell rings, Mom waves as we leave her classroom. "We'll start learning the songs for the show next week," she says. "And remember, you're all stars."

But I don't feel like a star. I feel like an eggplant.

On the way home from school, Joey can't stop talking about Fall Festival. "It will be so great," he says. "We can practice our parts together."

"I won't need to practice," I tell Joey. "All an eggplant does is lay in a bowl."

Joey shrugs. "You don't know what you'll have to do yet."

I don't know what I'll have to do, but I'm pretty sure I won't want to do it.

At dinner, I tell Mom I don't want to be an eggplant. "Don't you think as the daughter of the music teacher, I should get to be the farmer's wife or a rain fairy?"

Mom puts a piece of chicken on my plate. "Mallory, we drew out of a hat."

"It's the perfect role for you," says Max. "You kind of look like an eggplant."

I try to ignore Max. I watch Mom spoon mashed potatoes onto my plate. "Fall Festival will be fun," she says. "It's about working together with your classmates. I'm sure you'll enjoy it."

I shake my head.

Mom puts her arm around me. "You'll make a very cute eggplant," she says. "Why don't you write Mary Ann and invite her to come see you in Fall Festival?"

The last thing I want is for Mary Ann to see me dressed up like an eggplant. I cross my arms.

"C'mon, Sweet Potato," says Dad. "Where's that good old Mallory spirit?"

It used to be just Mom who called me Sweet Potato, but now Dad does it too.

I look inside my milk glass and underneath my placemat. "I can't find it anywhere!" I tell Dad. "So you might as well change my name from *Sweet* Potato to *Unhappy* Eggplant."

THE DAILY NEWS

"Calling all columnists." Mrs. Daily taps Chester on the head. "Would anyone here like to be in the newspaper business?"

Hands shoot up everywhere.

"Class, we're going to publish a newspaper for the whole school to read," says Mrs. Daily. "We'll publish one issue per month. Does anyone know the main function of a newspaper?"

Pamela's hand is up high. Mrs. Daily points to her.

"To give information to people," Pamela says.

"Excellent, Pamela." Mrs. Daily writes the word *information* on the chalkboard. "What kind of information do you think we should include in our newspaper?"

"Sports scores," Pete shouts.

"Horoscopes," Danielle and Arielle say together.

"Comics," says Zack.

"News," suggests Adam.

"Advice," says Emma.

Mrs. Daily writes *sports scores, horoscopes, comics, news,* and *advice* on the chalkboard. "I think we should include all of this information in our paper," she says.

Then she writes something else on the board—*Profile: A description of someone's abilities, personality, or career.*

"Class, we're going to learn how to write

profiles. We'll be picking one teacher at Fern Falls Elementary to write about for each issue of our paper. We'll call that our Teacher-of-the-Month column."

I raise my hand. "Mrs. Daily, how will we decide which teachers to write about?"

"Good question, Mallory. We'll pick Fern Falls Elementary teachers who are doing special things that other students might find interesting."

Pamela leans over to my side of the desk. "I'm going to tell Mrs. Daily we should pick her for the first issue. Students will find it interesting that we're writing a newspaper."

I'm not sure other students will think that's interesting, but I'm sure Mrs. Daily will like the idea. It bugs me that Pamela always says things Mrs. Daily likes hearing.

I rub my forehead with my pinkies.

Mary Ann and I used to do that when we were trying to think of something good to say.

Right now, I want to think of something to say that Mrs. Daily will like hearing.

"Now," says Mrs. Daily. "We need to pick a name for our paper. Any ideas?"

Everyone starts whispering. I keep rubbing.

Then I remember something Mom said.

"Maybe we should call it *The Daily News*," I whisper to Pamela. "Get it? Mrs. Daily. *Daily News*. Do you think Mrs. Daily will like that?"

Pamela's hand flies up in the air. "How about *The Daily News?*" she blurts out. She doesn't even wait for Mrs. Daily to call on her.

"Hmmm." Mrs. Daily rubs her chin. "It's catchy. Let's see a show of hands.

Who likes the name *The Daily News* for our newspaper?"

Hands shoot up everywhere.

"It's settled then." Mrs. Daily writes *The Daily News* in big, bold letters on the chalkboard. "Our newspaper will be called *The Daily News*. Let's all thank Pamela for the wonderful suggestion."

Everyone claps. Everyone but me.

PAMELA STOLE MY IDEA! I thought of something Mrs. Daily would like hearing and Pamela took the words right out of my mouth.

Everyone is busy talking about *The Daily News*. But not me. I'm busy trying to figure out what I want to say to Pamela.

And the answer is not much. I don't care if I ever speak to Pamela again.

"Settle down." Mrs. Daily taps Chester. "Everyone in this class will be part of the paper. I want each of you to give some thought to what you'd like to write."

What I'd like to write is a want ad:

WaNted.
New desk mate. Kind and friendly. THieves doN't apply. CoNtaCT MaLLORy McDoNaLd. FeRN FaLLs ELemeNtaRy. RooM 310. Row 2. Seat 6.

I tried giving Pamela a chance, but if you ask me, it was a flop. I can't believe she stole my idea. I always told Mary Ann my good ideas, and she never took them. I don't know if desk mates can officially not speak to each other, but I'm officially not speaking to Pamela.

"Now," says Mrs. Daily. "Unless someone can think of something else we should include in our newspaper, let's open our math books."

Joey raises his hand. "I can think of something else we should include. How about announcements?"

Mrs. Daily smiles. "What kind of announcements did you have in mind?"

"You know, stuff that's going on in school, like the date of the Fall Festival."

"Joey, that's a wonderful idea. *The Daily News* announcement column. I like it."

I don't! I don't want to announce Fall Festival to the whole school. Maybe Joey wants everyone to see him—he's Farmer Brown. But I don't want anyone to see me!

Mrs. Daily taps Chester on the head, and the classroom gets quiet.

"The newspaper will be lots of fun.

We'll start working on it next week. Class, please open your math textbooks to page sixty-two."

I open mine to page sixty-two. Word problems. Long, complicated word problems fill the page from top to bottom.

I sigh. Page sixty-two and I have a lot in common.

We're both full of problems.

LETTER
WRITING

I'm being held prisoner . . . by my mother! She says I have a lot of writing to do, and I can't go outside until I do it.

I have to write my article for *The Daily News,* and I have to write to Mary Ann and invite her to Fall Festival. I know why I have to write the article for *The Daily News.* It's due Monday. But I don't know why I have to write to Mary Ann.

Mom says there's nothing more exciting than getting an invitation in the mail. I told her I can think of a lot of things that are more exciting.

But Mom said she's been asking me to write this letter for over two weeks, and I'm stuck in my room until the letter and the article are written.

I pull out a sheet of paper. I'm going to write my article first.

On Friday, Pamela told me she'd be working on what she's writing for the newspaper *all* weekend. "Doesn't that sound like fun?" she asked me.

"Fun, fun, fun," I mumbled. But being stuck in my room writing doesn't sound like fun, fun, fun to me. I pick up Cheeseburger and put her on top of my desk.

Cheeseburger purrs and closes her eyes. But I open mine. Cheeseburger just gave me a great idea! I start writing. My article doesn't take long at all.

When I finish, I take out another sheet of paper so I can start on my letter. But getting started isn't easy.

I want to see Mary Ann, but I don't want Mary Ann to see me dressed up as an eggplant. I rub my forehead for a long time, and then I begin.

Dear Mary Ann,

Do you remember I told you that my mom is the new music teacher at my school? Well, she is making the third graders do a show called Fall Festival.

It is about a farmer and the vegetables on his farm. I am an eggplant in the show. It is a silly and babyish show!

Mom told me to write you a letter and invite you and your mom to come and see the show. YOU DEFINITELY DO NOT HAVE TO COME.

I want you to come and visit, but another time will be MUCH better.

If you have to sit through the show, you will be bored. Bored. Bored. Bored. So it

is probably best if you don't come for Fall
Festival.

    After you read this letter, rip it up and
forget I even sent it. OK?

    That's it.

    I hope you're eating lots of candy out of
Mrs. Thompson's jar. If I were in her class,
that's what I would be doing.

    G.2.G. (Got to go!)

    Hugs and Kisses, Mallory

I reread my letter. I really don't want
Mary Ann to come to Fall Festival.

I think back to the last practice. I
didn't even do anything until the end of
the show when I sang a song with a bunch
of other vegetables.

I don't know what the big deal is about
seeing me do that.

I reread my letter. Then I lick the
envelope shut and seal it with a kiss . . .
an *I-sure-hope-this-works-and-Mary-Ann-won't-
come-to-Fall-Festival* kiss.

TEACHER-OF-THE-MONTH

"IT'S OUT!" screams Pamela.

"What's out?" I check the floor around my desk. "A rat? A mouse? A snake?"

"No, silly." Pamela shoves the first issue of *The Daily News* in my face and starts jumping up and down like a cheerleader in the last minute of a tied game. "It's soooo exciting!" she squeals.

I walk to the front of the classroom and

get a copy of *The Daily News* off of Mrs.
Daily's desk. I search through the Table of
Contents until I find what I'm looking for. I
flip to page seven, cross my toes, and read.

HOW TO GET YOUR CAT TO NAP
by Mallory McDonald
(Dedicated to Cheeseburger, my cat, who is
a great napper)

Most cats love to nap. But if you
have the kind of cat that prefers to
be awake, here are some tips to get
your cat to sleep.

Tip #1: Sing your cat a lullaby.
(Don't try this if you sing off-key.
Your cat might get mad and stay
awake forever.)

Tip #2: Draw a picture for your

cat of other cats sleeping. (Once she sees that cats are doing this everywhere, she might want to try it herself.)

Tip #3: Make your cat watch while you do your homework. (I promise this will put your cat to sleep!)

Tip #4: If your cat is already sleeping (this is my best advice), DON'T WAKE HER UP!

If you need help with any of these tips, ask Mallory McDonald, local cat expert.

My article isn't bad. In fact, it's pretty good. Cats should be sleeping all over Fern Falls by the end of the day.

But I don't get a chance to admire it for long before Pamela starts squealing again. "Mal-lor-y, did you see my Teacher-of-the-Month column on page three?"

She looks over my shoulder and waits for me to read it.

Even though I'm officially not speaking to Pamela, I flip to page three and start reading.

TEACHER-OF-THE-MONTH:
Fern Falls Elementary Third Grade
Teacher, Mrs. Daily
by Pamela Brooks (her devoted student)

Mrs. Daily is the third grade teacher at Fern Falls Elementary.

Mrs. Daily makes learning fun! She makes learning science fun! She makes learning social studies fun! She makes learning math fun!

Mrs. Daily makes learning so much fun that even when you're learning, you feel like you're at recess!

Mrs. Daily is SUPER! It was her idea to publish this SUPER newspaper!

I asked Mrs. Daily if she could tell us the secret to her success as a teacher.

"You have to love what you do to do a good job at it, and I love what I do," says Mrs. Daily.

I love what she does too and so do a lot of third graders at Fern Falls Elementary.

So let's all give a big cheer for Mrs. Daily.

Hip, hip, hooray! Hip, hip, hooray! Hip, hip, hooray!

Thank you, Mrs. Daily, for being the best teacher ever!!!!!!!!!!!!!

I close my newspaper. I've read enough.

Pamela tugs on my sleeve. "Mrs. Daily said she looooved my article, and the apple I gave her for being Teacher-of-the-Month."

I roll my newspaper into a cone, in case I have to barf. I'm sure Mrs. Daily looooved Pamela's article and her apple. She loooooves everything Pamela does. But I don't! I reopen my newspaper and pretend to read the school lunch menus.

Mrs. Daily taps Chester on the head. "Class, you should be proud of the first issue of *The Daily News*. You all worked hard. Does anybody have any comments?"

Joey raises his hand. "Did everybody see my announcement column?"

I unroll my paper. Joey's announcement column is on page four. Dress rehearsal for Fall Festival is next Thursday night.

My last eggplant-free weekend.

I think about all the times we've practiced our songs in music class. It's one thing to sing like an eggplant but another thing to dress like one.

Pamela leans over my shoulder and reads the announcement column. "Dress rehearsal is next week. It's soooo exciting," she squeals. "Even though we've been practicing in class, won't it be exciting when we finally get to rehearse on the stage?"

I put my head on my desk and groan.

I'm trying to get excited. But some things are hard to get excited about.

Having Pamela Brooks as a desk mate is one of those things.

Being an eggplant in Fall Festival is another.

DRESS
REHEARSAL

"Eat your meatball," says Mom.

I push my plate away.

I don't want to eat my meatball. I also don't want to put on my eggplant costume and go to the auditorium tonight for dress rehearsal, and that's what I have to do as soon as I finish eating my meatball.

"C'mon," says Mom. "I can't be late."

I take a teeny tiny bite of meatball and spit it in my napkin. "This tastes funny."

"Mallory!" Mom says my name like I'm going to ruin the whole night if I don't eat what's on my plate.

Dad sticks his fork in the meatball on his plate and takes a bite. "New recipe?"

Mom puts a bowl of spaghetti on the table. "Actually, they're frozen. I've been so busy with Fall Festival, I haven't had time to cook."

I look at Mom. She's wearing a T-shirt that says *Director* on it. It should say *All I care about is this stinkin' show.* Fall Festival is ALL she cares about these days.

Mom looks at me. "Mallory, hurry up."

I stick a fork into my meatball and hold it up to the light. "Who invented frozen meatballs?"

Mom groans.

I continue inspecting my meatball. "Maybe the astronauts did. They kind of

look like moon rocks."

Max shoves a big bite in his mouth. "Who cares who invented them?" Max helps himself to two more meatballs. "They're great. You'd know if you'd eat yours."

Easy for Max to say. He doesn't care if he has to eat a frozen meatball, just like he doesn't care that Mom is the music teacher at our school. But Max and I are different, because I do care.

I take a teeny, tiny bite. Then I give Mom an *I'm-going-to-be-sick* look.

Mom takes my plate and dumps it in the garbage. "We don't have time for this," she says.

She picks up the phone and calls the Winston's. She tells Joey to come over because it's time to go.

"Tonight will be awesome," says Joey when we're in the van. "I can't wait to rehearse on stage. It will be really different from doing it in the classroom."

Mom smiles at him in the rearview mirror. When we pull into the parking lot, Mom asks Joey and me to carry an armload of costumes.

Mom follows us into the auditorium.

"Careful, Mallory," she says. "Your costumes are dragging. You don't want anything to happen to them, do you?"

"Actually, I do," I whisper to Joey. "I want them to drop off a cliff."

I wait for Joey to laugh. But he doesn't. "Mallory, you should change your attitude. Fall Festival will be lots of fun."

Fun for him . . . he has a great part. He didn't have to invite his best friend to come watch him.

When we get inside the auditorium, Mom starts spreading the costumes out on chairs. The auditorium is filling up with Fern Falls Elementary third graders.

"OK, everyone." Mom looks at her clipboard. "Let's get into these costumes."

Joey puts on a straw hat. Pamela ties a red-checkered apron around her waist. The townspeople roll up the hems of their blue jeans and tuck in their white T-shirts.

Fruits and vegetables are putting on their costumes. Produce is popping up everywhere. There's a peach, a plum, an apple, and a bowl of cherries. There's a carrot, a radish, a string bean, and two lettuce leaves.

Mom asks me to adjust the stem on a

cluster of grapes. Then she helps me step into my eggplant costume. She starts pinning on my stem.

"Hold still," she says. "I don't want to stick you."

"What would happen if you did?" I ask. "Would eggplant juice drip out?" I laugh at my joke.

But Mom doesn't.

Joey looks at me like I'm a circus monkey who won't cooperate with the trainer. "Be serious," he says. "Fall Festival is tomorrow night, and we have a lot of work to do."

Did I hear him right? Did Joey tell me to be serious? If you ask me, Joey is taking Fall Festival *way* too seriously.

"OK, everyone," says Mom. "I want to take a quick picture before we get started. Fruits in front, vegetables in the back, townspeople and farmers squat in the middle. Everybody smile and say *salad*!"

I think about the picture. If I make a scrapbook of Fall Festival, it will look more like a cookbook than a scrapbook.

Mom blows her whistle. "Places everyone. Let's stick to the schedule." She sits in the front row of the auditorium while we sing all our songs.

First, the farmer sings. Then his wife sings. Then the townspeople sing. Then the fruits make a singing fruit salad.

When the vegetables go on stage, I waddle behind Dawn the string bean. The vegetables make a circle around the lettuce leaves and sing our song.

What would you do if no one ate the stew?
How would you feel if you got a raw deal?
Everyone should eat at least five a day.
Ask any vegetable, and that's what they'll say.

When we're done, the lettuce leaves sing the salad finale.

"Bravo!" Mom shouts when they finish. "Tomorrow night will be a smashing success."

When I get home, I'm going to the wish pond to wish that somehow, some way, this show will close before it ever opens.

But when I get home, Max hands me a letter. "It's from Mary Ann," he says.

I rip it open and start reading.

Dear Mallory,

Mom says we wouldn't miss the Fall Festival for anything. We think you will make a very cute eggplant!!! We're driving up Friday after school so we'll get there in time for the show. But Mom says we have to drive back Saturday morning.

SEE YOU SO, SO, SO SOON!

CAN'T WAIT, WAIT, WAIT!

FALL FESTIVAL WILL BE THE BEST!

Hugs and Kisses, Mary Ann

I rub my eyes. I can't believe Mary Ann is coming to Fall Festival.

I crumple up her letter and aim for the trash. Max catches it midair and reads it. "For once, Birdbrain is right. You'll make an adorable eggplant."

"Be serious," I tell Max. "As my big brother, you could try to help me think of something so I won't look stupid on stage."

"You're right." Max hands me Mary Ann's letter. He looks serious. "How about dancing lessons?" Max puffs out his cheeks and dances around the room like an overgrown eggplant. Then he falls on the floor laughing.

I crumple up Mary Ann's letter and throw it in the trash. "I hope you laugh so hard your head falls off," I tell Max.

I run to my room and slam my door. But even after I do, I can still hear Max laughing.

And the truth is, I don't blame him. I'm sure the sight of *Mallory the Dancing Eggplant* live on stage will be just hilarious.

A BROKEN LEG

Joey and I stop and read the sign on the bulletin board outside the auditorium:

"Fall Festival Tonight," he says out loud.

I can tell reading that sign makes Joey feel terrific. But it makes me feel sick. I feel my head. I think I have a fever . . . Fall Festival Fever.

I know if I tell Mom, she'll just say, "The show must go on!" Max says that's "show talk." Lately, that's the only kind of talk I hear from Mom.

Backstage, Mom zips kids into costumes. "Who's excited for Fall Festival?" she asks.

This must be a trick question. Who could possibly be excited?

But I look around and see lots of kids who look excited—Joey, Pamela, even Zack and Adam, who are lettuce leaves, look excited.

I pull my eggplant stem down on my head. I think I'm the only one around here who's NOT. I waddle over to a chair and sit down.

I think about this afternoon when Mary Ann and her mom got to our house.

As soon as they pulled into the driveway, Mary Ann popped out of the car and started hugging me like crazy.

"You're going to be a star!" She was jumping and dancing around me. She even tried to pick me up. "I know a stage star! I know a stage star!"

"Cut it out," I mumbled to Mary Ann.

But her mom heard me. "She's just excited to see you onstage tonight, and so am I." She rumpled my hair. "We wouldn't drive three hours to see anybody but you."

Then Mary Ann started jumping all over me again. "I want to see your costume!"

So I took Mary Ann to my room and showed her my costume.

"Try it on," she squealed.

I modeled my costume for Mary Ann. "I look ridiculous, don't I?" I was hoping Mary Ann would say, *"No, you look really, really, really cute."*

But that's not what she said. She didn't say anything . . . she couldn't, because she couldn't stop laughing!

I crossed my arms across my chest.

"Look." Mary Ann was trying to keep a

straight face. "It could be worse. You could have been an onion or a turnip. At least your costume is a good color."

But I could tell Mary Ann didn't think there was anything *good* about it.

Backstage, I wiggle in my chair and straighten my stem. Crowd noises are starting to fill the auditorium.

I pretend like I'm at the wish pond and make a wish: *I wish there was some way I could get out of this show.* But I don't think wishing will do much good.

Mom claps her hands. "Listen up, everybody. The show starts in just a few minutes, so find your places backstage."

I walk to my place near the front curtain and peek at the auditorium. It's filling up with people. I see Dad, Mary Ann, her mom.

As Mom says, *The show must go on.* But I can't wait until it's over.

"One minute till showtime," says Mom. "Quiet everyone."

Someone pulls the stem on top of my eggplant hat. I turn around. It's Max.

"What are you doing back here?" I whisper.

"I wanted to tell you to break a leg."

"Huh?" I can't believe my own brother wants me to break a leg!

"It's show talk." Max gives me a thumbs-up sign. "It means good luck on stage."

Max goes, but he leaves me with an idea . . . a thumbs-up idea. If I pretend like I broke my leg, I won't have to be *Mallory the Dancing Eggplant.*

That's it! All I have to do is find the right time to pretend like I broke it.

"Showtime," says Mom. "Concentrate and have fun."

I am concentrating . . . on breaking my leg. I've never broken a leg before. I've

never even pretended to break one.

Joey goes on stage first. He reads a page from Farmer Brown's journal about how much he loves his farm and his fruits and vegetables.

He sings a song, "No One Gives a Hoot about Veggies and Fruit."

When he's finished, the audience claps.

I squirm. I can't break my leg just standing here.

Then it's Pamela's turn. She reads a poem about wanting to save the farm. She sings "Let's Have a Feast." More clapping. Still no chance to break a leg.

When the townspeople go on stage, they sing "We Love Junk Food."

I watch a peach, a plum, an apple, some grapes, and a bowl of cherries go on stage. I listen as they sing the song they've practiced in music class.

Fruit, glorious fruit.
We hope you will try it.
Three pieces a day
Makes a healthy diet.
Just picture a great big peach—
Plump, juicy, and cute.
Oh fruit! Glorious fruit,
Glorious fruit, glorious fruit.

I wish I could find a glorious way to break my leg.

Emma the peach holds up a sign for the audience that says, *GO BANANAS!* There's clapping and whistling, just like Mom said there would be.

Still no chance for me to break a leg.

Mom motions for the vegetables to go on stage.

I follow a carrot, a potato, a radish, a string bean, and two lettuce leaves on stage. The vegetables make a circle around the lettuce leaves.

I walk to the back of the circle. Then I see it—the crate! Onstage, there's a little crate I'm supposed to stand on while we sing.

It's the chance I've been waiting for. All I have to do is pretend to trip when I'm stepping onto the crate, and I won't have to do my part in the show.

I walk toward the crate. Two more steps. I take a deep breath, close my eyes, and step up. I hope this works.

I pretend to trip and fall on the floor. "AAARGH! My leg! It's broken!"

It's not easy to clutch your leg and roll around in pain when you're wrapped up in five yards of purple felt, but I do.

Mom runs onto the stage. The vegetables turn around to see what's going on. Everybody in the auditorium is looking at me, and that's the one thing I didn't want anybody to be looking at!

Mom pokes my leg. "Can you move it?"

"Oooh!" I moan like people do on TV when they're really hurt and wiggle my ankle. "Just a little," I whisper.

Mom helps me stand up. "Let's go backstage and put ice on it. The show can continue." Mom motions the vegetables to start without me. Backstage, I sit in a chair.

Mom inspects my leg. "Are you OK?"

"I think so." I adjust the ice pack and watch while everybody does the finale

we've been practicing in music class since the second week of school.

But Mom isn't watching the finale. She's watching me. "Don't you want to see the end of the show?" I ask her. She shakes her head.

Part of me is glad I'm not on stage singing, but part of me wishes I was. It would be better than sitting back here with Mom staring at me.

Clapping fills the auditorium. The show is over. Everyone comes backstage.

Pamela gives Mom flowers. "Thank you, Mrs. McDonald," she says. "This was the best Fall Festival ever."

Joey puts his fingers in his mouth, whistles, and yells "Yee-haw!" He sounds more like a cowboy than a farmer, but everybody laughs.

"I'm proud of all of you," says Mom.

"You did a wonderful job. There's a party in the auditorium. Punch and cookies for everyone."

Kids start running to the refreshment table. Everyone looks like they feel great.

Almost everyone. My leg is fine, but the rest of me feels awful. I thought I would feel good if I didn't have to be in the show, but now I wish Mom was saying she was proud of me too. I stay in my chair and hold the ice pack on my leg.

People start crowding around me. Dad, Joey, Pamela. Even though they ask if I'm OK, I feel like they all know what they're looking at . . . a leg that's not broken.

"Way to ruin a show," Max whispers in my ear. Winnie is standing behind him with her arms crossed. "My brother's chance at stardom washed down the drain."

I ignore Winnie and rearrange my ice

pack. "Max, you're the one who told me to break my leg!"

"Show talk, remember?" says Max.

Mary Ann brings me some punch and cookies. She hands me the plate, but I put it down. I love punch and cookies, but I'm not in the mood for a party.

When we get home, Mom takes out towels for Mary Ann and her mom.

"Maybe your family needs a few minutes alone," says Mary Ann's mom.

Mom nods her head like that's exactly what we need. "Mallory, you and Mary Ann get ready for bed, then Dad and I would like to see you in our room."

I pull on my flower power pajamas.

"I brought the same ones." Mary Ann pulls hers on too. She flips her head over and brushes her hair. "Too bad we didn't get to see you perform tonight."

I sit down on the floor, beside Mary Ann. I always know what I want to say to my best friend, but right now, I'm not so sure.

Mary Ann stops brushing. "I think your mom wants to talk about what happened tonight."

I want to talk about it too, and I do. I tell Mary Ann about all the things that have changed in my life since I started school in Fern Falls.

I tell her how hard it has been to start a new school.

I tell her that it hasn't been much fun taking Mom with me.

I tell her Mom doesn't have much time to be my mom, like she used to.

Mary Ann sits down on the bed beside me. "Remember when my parents got divorced? Everything changed. And then after a while, I got used to it."

I think about what Mary Ann said. "Do you think I'll ever get used to the way things are now?"

Mary Ann nods and smiles.

Max sticks his head in my room. "News flash: you're in big trouble! You better get upstairs on the double!"

Max is right. I slip my feet into my fuzzy duck slippers and trudge upstairs to Mom and Dad's room. I feel like I'm entering the

Chamber of Doom.

Mom tells me to sit on the bed. She crosses her arms. "Mallory, I know you weren't excited about the show. Did you fall on purpose?"

When I swallow, I feel like I've got a cement truck stuck in my throat.

I wish I could be anywhere but here right now in a junkyard, a sewer plant, even

a swamp filled with quicksand and hungry alligators.

I nod. It's a tiny nod, but it's big enough for Mom to know the truth.

She shakes her head. "Mallory, what you did was wrong. You let your classmates down. You let the audience down. You let me down."

Mom keeps talking. "Sometimes we all have to do things we don't want to do, and that's what you should have done. Sometimes we have to consider other people's feelings, not just our own."

My feet feel cold, even inside my fuzzy duck slippers.

Mom is quiet for a minute, but her face is all pinched up, like a raisin. "Mallory, is there something you'd like to say?"

Actually, there are a lot of things I'd like to say. I think about the expressionist paintings we're working on in art class. It's easy to paint how you feel. But it's harder to say it when someone's staring at you with crossed arms and an angry look on her face.

"I'm sorry," I mumble.

Parents should know it's embarrassing to get in trouble when you have a friend over. "Mary Ann is waiting for me downstairs," I tell them.

"I think we've talked enough for one night," says Dad. He and Mom kiss me good night. But I can tell what they're really thinking is *bad night*.

And I agree. This was a very, very, very bad night.

AT THE WISH POND

I look through the stones on the edge of the wish pond. I'd like to find a wish pebble. The problem is they're never around when you need one.

"Doughnut for your thoughts," says Dad. He sits down next to me and opens a box of chocolate doughnuts with colored sprinkles.

I shake my head. I love doughnuts, but this morning, I'm not in the mood.

Dad puts the box down and picks through the rocks on the edge of the pond.

"What are you looking for?" I ask.

Dad doesn't answer. He keeps picking through the rocks.

"If you're looking for a wish pebble, you might as well give up," I tell him. "They're pretty hard to find."

"No," says Dad. "I'm not looking for a wish pebble." He stops digging through the rocks and looks at me. "I'm looking for the Mallory I know who always works at something until things work out the way she'd like them to."

Dad smiles. "Lately, she's been pretty hard to find."

I kick my toe in the water. "You're not going to find her under a rock."

Dad hands me a doughnut. "I peeked into your room this morning. Mary Ann was still asleep, and your bed was empty. I thought you might be out here."

I pick a sprinkle off my doughnut.

"Feel like talking?" asks Dad.

I shake my head from side to side.

Dad looks at the pile of stones in my lap. "Well, since this is a wish pond, I bet you came out here to make some wishes. Am I right about that?"

I shake my head up and down.

"Feel like telling me what you plan to wish for?"

"If I tell you, my wishes might not come true."

Dad puts his arm around me and pulls me close to him. "Sweet Potato, it might help to talk about what's bothering you."

I hadn't planned to talk, but everything

that's bothering me starts popping out of my mouth like kernels flying out of the popcorn machine at the movies.

"I wish I was still at my old school with Mary Ann.

"I wish things with Joey were like they were this summer.

"I wish Mom hadn't picked a stupid theme for Fall Festival.

"I wish she hadn't made me invite Mary Ann to see the show.

"I wish things could be like they used to be before Mom was a teacher.

"And what I really wish is that I could make her not mad at me anymore."

"Phew." Dad takes a deep breath. "That's a pretty long list. Got any ideas how you might make some of those wishes come true?"

I shrug.

Dad pulls me closer to him. "Feel like hearing a story?"

I shrug again. I know Dad will tell his story, whether I want to hear it or not.

"Once upon a time there was a little girl," says Dad. "She loved to play with blocks. She used to build all kinds of things out of blocks. She would build houses and schools and boats and even cities out of blocks.

"Now this little girl had an older brother. One day, her brother used her blocks to build a tower. He built a big, tall tower with all the blocks. When he was finished, his tower stood straight and tall, almost as tall as the little girl.

"The little girl must have decided to herself that building a big, tall tower looked like fun because that's what she started to do."

Dad pauses and looks at me. "But she soon found out that building big, tall towers wasn't as easy as it looked. Every time her tower started to get tall, it fell over.

"But the little girl didn't stop building. For weeks, she kept building towers. Every time her tower fell over, she started over again until, finally, she built a big, tall block tower with all of her blocks, just like the one her older brother had built."

Dad is quiet for a minute. He picks up a handful of stones from the edge of the wish pond and starts stacking them one on top of the other, until they topple over.

"Building towers isn't easy. But the little girl stuck with it until she did it." Dad looks at me. "I knew right then and there that this little girl would always keep trying until she accomplished what she set out to do."

I throw a rock in the water. "Are you talking about me?"

Dad nods.

"Now my problems are bigger than building a tower out of blocks."

"And you're bigger now than the little girl in the story," says Dad. "I'm sure if you'll just give yourself and everyone around you a chance, you'll find a way to make things just the way you'd like them to be. You always have, and I know you always will."

Dad stands up and hands me the box of doughnuts. "I'm going home now. Why don't you take a few minutes to think before the day gets started."

After Dad leaves, I take another doughnut out of the box. So much has changed since we moved. Things aren't the way I'd like them to be. Especially things with Mom.

I think about the conversation I had with Mom and Dad last night. Actually, it wasn't a conversation because I didn't do any talking. Mom did it all.

There were things I wanted to say, like I wish she had considered someone's feelings besides her own . . . MINE! But all I did was mumble *I'm sorry*.

And I am sorry. Sorry I was ever born.

I think Mom would be a whole lot happier if she didn't have a daughter at the school where she teaches. Then she could say to people: *Meet my ONLY child Max. He's a bright, happy fifth grader. He plays baseball. He eats frozen meatballs. And he doesn't mind that I teach music at his school.*

I know Mom was really upset last night. Even though part of me is mad at Mom, all of her is mad at me, and I don't like it when she is mad at me.

I tear off a piece of doughnut and toss it into the water.

I wish I could do something so Mom wouldn't be mad anymore.

"MALLORY!" Mom yells from down the street. "COME ON, MARY ANN AND HER MOM ARE LEAVING IN A FEW MINUTES."

I bet Mom wanted to say: *"Pack a bag and you can go with them."*

I stand up and throw the rest of my doughnut into the pond.

I think about what Dad said, about finding a way to make things how I want them to be. But I think no matter what I do, Mom will still be mad at me.

I think the best thing for me to do is to look in the yellow pages this afternoon and see if I can find a new mom.

PART OF A PLAN

When I get to school on Monday morning, I feel like everyone is thinking the same thing: there goes the eggplant who didn't really break her leg.

I walk to my classroom and sit down at my desk.

Pamela is already in her seat. She smiles at me. It looks like a *good-morning-my-mom-told-me-I-had-to-be-nice-to-you-even-though-you-ruined-Fall-Festival* smile.

Mrs. Daily taps Chester. "Class, please

open your science books to chapter five."

I flip to chapter five. Bears. Bears have it easy. They don't have to go to school. They don't have to be in shows. I'd like to be a bear.

"Joey, please read for us," says Mrs. Daily.

Joey reads. "Bears can be found throughout the world. They are large mammals with thick, coarse fur and short tails. Bears walk flat on the soles of their

feet. Black bears, brown bears, and polar bears are three of the most well-known types of bears."

If I were a bear, I'm not sure which kind I'd want to be.

"Sammy, will you please continue," asks Mrs. Daily.

Sammy takes over where Joey left off.

"Bears spend the winter months asleep or in an inactive condition called hibernation. They emerge from their caves in the spring, in late March or April."

Now I know what kind of bear I want to be . . . the kind that hibernates.

I could go to sleep now and wake up in March. By then, everybody would forget about the eggplant who didn't really break her leg at Fall Festival . . . especially Mom.

I wonder if there are any caves in Fern Falls.

While I'm busy planning my hibernation, Pamela passes me a note. It says *this concerns you* on the outside. I'm not speaking to Pamela, but when I get a *this-concerns-you* note, I want to read it. I unfold the paper.

Mallory, I have a plan. YOU ARE PART OF THIS PLAN!!!! Meet me under the monkey bars at recess. I'll explain then. I KNOW you will like it. When the bell rings, HURRY! We have a LOT to talk about. YOU HAVE TO COME!
Your friend, Pamela

I can't imagine what Pamela has in mind. I look at her, but she moves her fingers across her lips like she's zipping them shut.

Pamela and I haven't been what you'd call friends since she stole my idea. But still, part of me wants to know what her plan is.

I think about what Dad said to me at the wish pond, about giving other people a chance. Maybe I should give Pamela a chance.

When the recess bell rings, I do *eenie, meenie, miney, mo.* I squeeze my palm and decide to . . . GO.

Pamela is waiting under the monkey bars when I get to the playground.

When I walk over to the monkey bars, Pamela looks at me. She looks nervous.

I feel like I should say something, but I haven't said anything to Pamela for a long time, so I don't know what to say.

Pamela faces me and folds her hands in her lap. "Mallory, your mom seemed pretty upset with you last night."

"So?" I shrug. I don't know why Pamela cares if Mom is mad at me.

"Well, I think I know a way to get her unmad."

"Huh?" I raise my eyebrows. I'd like to find a way to get Mom unmad at me.

"Why don't we ask Mrs. Daily if you can write the next Teacher-of-the-Month column about your mom?"

Pamela leans toward me like she's telling me a secret she doesn't want anyone else to hear. "Since your mom just did Fall Festival, kids will think it's interesting to learn more about her. You can say how sorry you are about what happened, and when she reads it in the paper, she won't be mad anymore."

I consider Pamela's plan.

"Tomorrow is the last day to submit

articles for the next issue," Pamela continues. "Why don't we go talk to Mrs. Daily before recess is over."

Even though I'm still a little mad at Pamela, I think her plan is a good one. "That sounds great. I think it's really nice that you want to help me, but I guess I don't understand why you want to."

I look down at some grass growing under the corner of the monkey bars. "After all, I did ruin Fall Festival."

Pamela picks at a blade of grass. "We all make mistakes. I'm sorry I took your idea for *The Daily News*," she says. "I'd like to be friends."

I didn't think I would ever smile again, but I do. "I'd like to be friends too."

"Do you want to come over to my house after school?" asks Pamela. "You can write your article. I'll help if you want."

I nod my head. "Sure."

"Um, maybe it's not such a good idea," says Pamela.

Uh-oh. I hope we don't stop being friends before we get started. "How come?"

"Well," says Pamela. "My sister Amanda will want to do everything with us. She won't leave us alone long enough to write the article. She can be a real pain sometimes."

"I've got a big brother, and he's always a pain. But I can't believe little sisters can be annoying."

Pamela laughs. "Believe it! I can't believe you didn't know that."

I guess there are lots of things about Pamela I didn't know.

"Hey," I say. "Why don't I bring my purple nail polish to your house, and Amanda can paint her fingernails while we write the article."

"Great idea. Amanda will love that." Pamela grabs my hand. "We better go talk to Mrs. Daily before we miss our chance."

We run back to the classroom.

I can't help thinking about what Dad said: *Sometimes you just have to give people a chance.* I'm glad I gave one to Pamela.

MOM-OF-
THE-MONTH

"It's out!" I scream. I clutch *The Daily News* with one hand and cover my eyes with the other.

Pamela grabs the paper out of my hand. "Open your eyes, silly."

I peek . . . just a little. "Don't you know how hard it is to read your own work?"

Pamela laughs. "That's only when it's bad." She starts reading aloud.

TEACHER-OF-THE-MONTH:
Fern Falls Elementary music
teacher, Mrs. McDonald
by Mallory McDonald (her loving and only
daughter)

Mrs. McDonald is a new face to
many of the students at Fern Falls
Elementary, but she's not new to
me. She's been my mom for 8¾
years, my entire life.

When she was a piano teacher at
home, she taught one student at a
time. But now that she's the music
teacher at Fern Falls Elementary,
she teaches lots of students.

I was really worried when I found
out she was going to be the music
teacher at my school. I thought she
wouldn't have time to be a mom and

a teacher. I thought I was losing a mom, but I realized what I gained was a great music teacher.

She's the world's best music teacher for lots of reasons.

She doesn't laugh at kids who sing off-key. She doesn't ask questions about composers who died a gazillion years ago. But best of all, Mrs. McDonald loves all kids and vegetables equally, even rotten ones (who are very, very, very sorry for any bad behavior and promise to be good from now on).

As a music teacher and a mom, Mrs. McDonald gets an A+. Mrs. McDonald is not only the Teacher-of-the-Month. She's the Mom-of-the-Month too.

Pamela folds the paper closed. "It's great," she says. "Your mom will love it."

I cross my fingers. I hope Pamela is right.

Even though she says she's not, I can tell Mom is still mad at me.

On Saturday, she made me clean out my drawers.

On Sunday, she didn't make peanut butter marshmallow pancakes. She always makes them for me on Sundays, and this Sunday, I got plain old pancakes.

And ever since Fall Festival, she's been calling me by my full name, Mallory Louise McDonald. The only time she calls me by my full name is when she's mad.

I hope Mom likes the article, and I hope she'll really forgive me for ruining Fall Festival. I don't know how I'm going to be able to wait until music class to see if Mom liked my article.

Mrs. Daily taps Chester on the head. "Class, take your seats and open your social studies books to page eighty-seven."

I open my book to a picture of Christopher Columbus.

"It took Christopher Columbus over two months to sail across the ocean with the Nina, the Pinta, and the Santa Maria to get to the New World," says Mrs. Daily.

"It took years to put his plan into place and see it through to completion. So you can see," says Mrs. Daily, "some plans take a very long time to work."

I hope my plan works faster than Christopher Columbus's did.

After social studies, Mrs. Daily says to take out our science books.

Someone knocks on the door.

"Class, please start reading on page sixty-one." She walks outside and shuts the door behind her.

I start reading, but Mrs. Daily cracks the door open. "Mallory, may I see you."

Uh-oh . . . whoever was talking to Mrs. Daily must have been talking about me! What if Mom's not the only one who's mad about Fall Festival? What if it's the principal and I'm in BIG trouble?

I walk outside . . . slowly.

But when I get outside, I'm surprised. It's not the principal . . . it's my mom.

"Mallory, your mother would like to have a word with you." Mrs. Daily winks at Mom then smiles at me. "Your article was excellent," she says.

Mrs. Daily goes back into the classroom.

I wish I could follow her inside. I'm not sure what Mom is doing here. There's a copy of *The Daily News* in her hand. I can't tell if she's happy or mad.

I cross my toes. "Did you like the article?"

Mom puts her arm around me. "What do you say we discuss it over lunch? How does McDonald's sound?"

Mom is taking me out for lunch? I get to go to McDonald's? She knows all McDonalds love McDonald's.

Mom is quiet in the car. When we sit down, I unwrap my cheeseburger and take a bite. But Mom doesn't touch her food.

"Mallory, what you did at the Fall Festival was wrong, and I think you know that."

I nod my head.

"I don't think you'll do anything like that again."

I nod my head again.

"And I know you're sorry that you ruined a special night for a lot of people."

I keep nodding. I hope I don't throw up my cheeseburger from all this nodding.

Mom spreads *The Daily News* on the table and turns to the page with my article on it. "But this is wonderful." She smiles at me.

Phew. I think it's safe to stop nodding. "Mom, I'm sorry I pretended to break my leg. I wish I hadn't ruined the show."

Mom takes a sip of her shake. "Is there anything else you'd like to say?"

Actually, there is. There are a lot of things I'd like to say. I take a deep breath.

"I didn't want you to be the music teacher at my school. I didn't want you to pick the theme you picked for Fall Festival. And I didn't want Mary Ann to come see the show. I tried to tell you, but you didn't listen to anything I had to say."

I feel like I've said enough, but for some reason, I keep going. "It's hard to share your mom with a whole school, especially when you're used to having her to yourself. It's not that being an eggplant was so bad, but I felt like you were spending so much time planning Fall Festival, you barely had time to be my mom. You even gave us frozen meatballs. You never gave us frozen meatballs before you were a teacher."

Mom is quiet for a minute. "Mallory, just because I gave you frozen meatballs doesn't mean I love you less. And I'll try to listen to what you have to say from now on. But sometimes things happen that you might not like. When they do, you might find they're not all that bad if you just give them a chance."

I take a sip of my shake. I think about Pamela. I gave her a chance, and I'm glad I did. Maybe Mom is right. "I'll try," I tell her.

Mom looks at me in a happy way, like she just ate an extra-salty french fry.

"Mallory, I'm proud of you. You did a good job telling me how you feel and you wrote a wonderful article. Sometimes we all have a tough time saying what's on our minds, and you expressed yourself beautifully."

Thinking about what Mom said makes me feel happy. I wonder if this is how Vincent Van Gogh felt when he painted.

Expressionism is starting to make more sense to me.

"Mom, there's something else I want to say."

Mom puts down her milk shake, and looks at me like what I have to say is important to her. "What's that?" she asks.

"I'm getting used to Fern Falls Elementary. I even think there are some fun parts to having you teach at the same school."

"Oh yeah?" Mom raises an eyebrow. "Which parts do you think are fun?"

I take a big bite of my cheeseburger. "The eating lunch at McDonald's part." I lean forward and whisper so no one but Mom can hear me. "It's a lot more fun than eating in that stinky cafeteria."

Mom looks around the restaurant and leans forward. "I think the cafeteria is stinky too. But I'll tell you a secret if you promise not to tell."

I nod.

"I keep a secret stash of candy bars in my desk. Sometimes I just need to eat something sweet to get that cafeteria smell out of my nose. You're welcome to stop by my room if you think a little bit of candy might help you too."

Going to lunch at McDonald's, access to a secret candy stash . . . having Mom as a teacher might be even better than I thought it would be.

"Sounds like a plan," I tell Mom.

We smile and dip our french fries in the ketchup cup at the same time.

HAPPY HALLOWEEN!

Someone sits down on my bed and rubs my back.

"Guess who?" says a voice.

Even though I'm covered with covers, I don't have to guess. I know it's Mom.

She tickles my back. "Rise and shine, Sleepyhead. It's Halloween!" Then she whispers in my ear. "I have a Halloween surprise for you. Candy corn pancakes . . .

your favorite!"

I sit up. "I have a surprise for you too. I'm not going to be a witch this year."

Mom is quiet for a minute. "But you're always a witch on Halloween. If you're not going to be a witch, what are you going to be?"

I smile at Mom. "That's another surprise."

When I finish my pancakes, I ask Mom if I can borrow the aluminum foil. I take it into my room and close the door. I get out paints and poster board and string and scissors and glue. Joey and Pamela are coming over, and we're making Halloween costumes.

After I set everything up, I go outside to wait for my friends.

When they arrive, we go into my room.

Max follows us. "What's going on in here?"

"You'll find out soon enough." I lock my door.

"So what do we do?" asks Joey. "I've never made my own costume."

Pamela looks through all the art supplies on the floor of my room. "Actually, neither have I." She smiles at me. "Mallory, you have to tell us where to start."

I smile at both of them. I know exactly where to start.

We spend the morning cutting, pasting, and coloring.

When Joey and Pamela and I finish gluing the last pieces on our costumes, we punch holes in the tops, tie strings through the holes, and slip them over our heads.

I spin around so they can see me. "What do you think?"

"I think no one else in Fern Falls will be dressed like us," says Joey.

"I think we're ready," says Pamela. We all nod and march into the kitchen to model our costumes for Mom and Max.

Mom gasps when she sees us. Even Max looks like he's impressed.

"What do you think?" I ask.

Mom grins. "Three Musketeers, very clever."

Max walks around us in a circle like he's a costume inspector. "Not bad," he says to Joey and Pamela. He stops in front of me. "Pretty good costume. Just try not to break a leg while you're wearing it."

Everybody laughs. Even Mom.

She takes her camera out of the drawer. "Get together, guys."

We put our arms around each other.

Mom says, "Say Happy Halloween," and snaps our picture.

"See you tonight," I tell Joey and Pamela.

They're going home and coming back to my house tonight to trick-or-treat. "Six o'clock sharp and don't be late. We have a lot of houses to go to!"

After they leave, Mom hands me an envelope. "This came for you this morning."

It's from Mary Ann! She wrote *HAPPY HALLOWEEN!* on the outside in big black and orange letters. I take her letter to my room and open it.

Dear Mallory,

HAPPY HALLOWEEN!

What are you going to be for Halloween this year?

Even though we won't be together, I'm going to be a witch, just like always. BUT HALLOWEEN WON'T BE THE SAME THIS YEAR!

Not without you or Cheeseburger. I won't have anybody to glue on fake black fingernails with. I won't have anybody to trade candy with. I won't even have a cat to go with my costume. Nobody will be able to say, "Which witch are you?"

Here's a Halloween poem for you:

Boo-Hoo! Boo-Hoo! Boo-Hoo!

Halloween won't be the same without you.

Hugs, hugs, hugs!

Kisses, kisses, kisses!

Mary Ann

I reread Mary Ann's letter. Then I take out my Halloween scrapbook and paste Mary Ann's letter in it. I leave enough room on the page to put in the picture Mom took of Joey, Pamela, and me.

This Halloween will be different from all my other Halloweens.

I used to go trick-or-treating with Mary Ann. Then we'd go back to her house and put our candy in a big bowl and share it all until it was gone. Some years, we got enough candy to last until Christmas.

This Halloween, I'm trick-or-treating with Joey and Pamela . . . *and* Winnie and Max are coming too. Max has never trick-or-treated with me, but when he heard that Winnie was coming, he decided to come along.

When we finish, we're meeting at the wish pond for a party. Joey says Halloween at the wish pond is a Wish Pond Road tradition.

I think about the wish pond. I've spent a lot of time there lately making a lot of wishes. And I've noticed something: sometimes my wishes come true, sometimes they don't, and sometimes they take a while to work.

I guess what Mom says is true: you have to give things a chance . . . even wishes.

I pull a sheet of paper out of my desk drawer.

Dear Mary Ann,
HAPPY HALLOWEEN TO YOU TOO!
I know you will be a very cute witch. Cheeseburger and I will both miss being part of the costume. You are right about one thing—HALLOWEEN WON'T BE THE

SAME THIS YEAR . . . not without you!

Believe it or not, I'm not going to be a witch this year.

At first, I thought I would be a witch because I'm always a witch with you. But I decided to try something different.

So you'll never guess what I'm going to be—a Three Musketeer. Not the sword fighter kind, the candy bar kind. Joey, Pamela, and I are going trick-or-treating together as The Three Musketeers.

It was my idea. When I told Joey about it, he said he wanted to go as a soccer player. So I told Joey that something was bugging me. I told him that I felt like he only wanted to be my friend some of the time, not all of the time.

I even told him that Max said he was just my "street friend." (Max says a "street friend" is someone who lives on your street and only wants to be friends at home.)

Joey said it was silly that Max said that. (Most of the stuff Max says is silly.)

Joey said friends can be different and still be friends. Then he said the more he thought about the candy bar idea, the more he liked it and to count him in.

When I told Pamela the idea, she said she LOVED IT! She even told Mrs. Daily about it (she made her promise not to tell anyone), and Pamela told her it was my idea.

Mrs. Daily told me she thought it was a delightfully sweet idea!

That's all for now. I have to go help Dad hang Halloween decorations in our yard. HAVE FUN TONIGHT! EAT LOTS OF CANDY!

I'm going to even though I know what Mom is going to say: "Don't eat too many sweets. You don't want to get a tummy ache before you go to bed."

But I know exactly what I'm going to tell her.

I'm going to tell her not to worry... because I like sweet endings!

Ha! Ha! Ha! Get the joke? Sweets. Sweet endings.

Happy, Happy, Happy Halloween!!!

Extra, Extra, Extra Big Huge Hugs and Kisses,

Mallory

CLASS PICTURES

Oh yeah! I almost forgot... next week we're taking class pictures and I can't decide what to wear. Mary Ann and I used to always help each other pick out just the right outfits, but since she's not here this year, I asked a few other people.

Dad said I should ask Mom. He said he's "no good" in the *picking-clothes* department. Mom said as long as I smile and say, "Cheese," I'll be fine. But Mom knows I always say, "Cheeseburger," when I take a picture.

Max said I should wear a paper bag over my head. Joey said he had no idea what I should wear. Winnie said it wouldn't matter, and Pamela said we should ask Mrs. Daily.

None of these people were any help at all. But maybe you can be. What do you think I should wear?

Me in bell bottoms
and a hippie top

Me in a mini
skirt and a
turtle neck

Me in jeans
and a poncho

Me in boots
and a sweater
dress

It is so hard to pick just the right outfit
for a class picture. Thanks so, so, so much
for your help!

The illustrator wishes to thank the St. Vincent Ferrer class of 2009!

A partial reproduction of the painting, "Still Life: Vase with Twelve Sunflowers (Bayerische Staatsgemäldesammlungen, Neue Pinakothek, Munich) by Vincent van Gogh is reflected on page 37.

Carolrhoda Books, Inc.
A division of Lerner Publishing Group
241 First Avenue North
Minneapolis, MN 55401 U.S.A.

Website address: www.carolrhodabooks.com

Library of Congress Cataloging-in-Publication Data

Friedman, Laurie B.,
    Back to school, Mallory / by Laurie Friedman; illustrations by Tamara
Schmitz.
        p.   cm.
    Summary: After moving, eight-year-old Mallory struggles with being new at school, especially because her mother is now the music teacher and director of the third grade play.
    ISBN: 1-57505-658-5 (lib. bdg. : alk. paper)
    [1. Moving, Household—Fiction. 2. First day of school—Fiction. 3. Schools—Fiction. 4. Family life—Fiction.] I. Schmitz, Tamara, ill. II. Title.
    PZ7.F89773Bac 2004
    [Fic]—dc22   2003018043

Manufactured in the United States of America
1 2 3 4 5 6 — BP — 09 08 07 06 05 04